Sammy Claws

The Christmas Cat

First published 2018 by Nosy Crow Ltd
The Crow's Nest, 14 Baden Place, Crosby Row, London SE1 1YW
www.nosycrow.com

Sammy Claws: The Christmas Cat
Text copyright © 2018 by Lucy Rowland
Illustrations copyright © 2018 by Paula Bowles
All rights reserved. Manufactured in China.
No part of this book may be used or reproduced in any manner whatsoever
without written permission except in the case of brief quotations embodied in
critical articles and reviews. For information address HarperCollins Children's
Books, a division of HarperCollins Publishers, 195 Broadway, New York, NY 10007.
www.harpercollinschildrens.com

ISBN 978-0-06-295911-9

19 20 21 22 23 WKT 10 9 8 7 6 5 4 3 2 1
First US Edition, 2019

For Billy and Charlotte xx
L. R.

For Mr. and Mrs. Claus x
P. B.

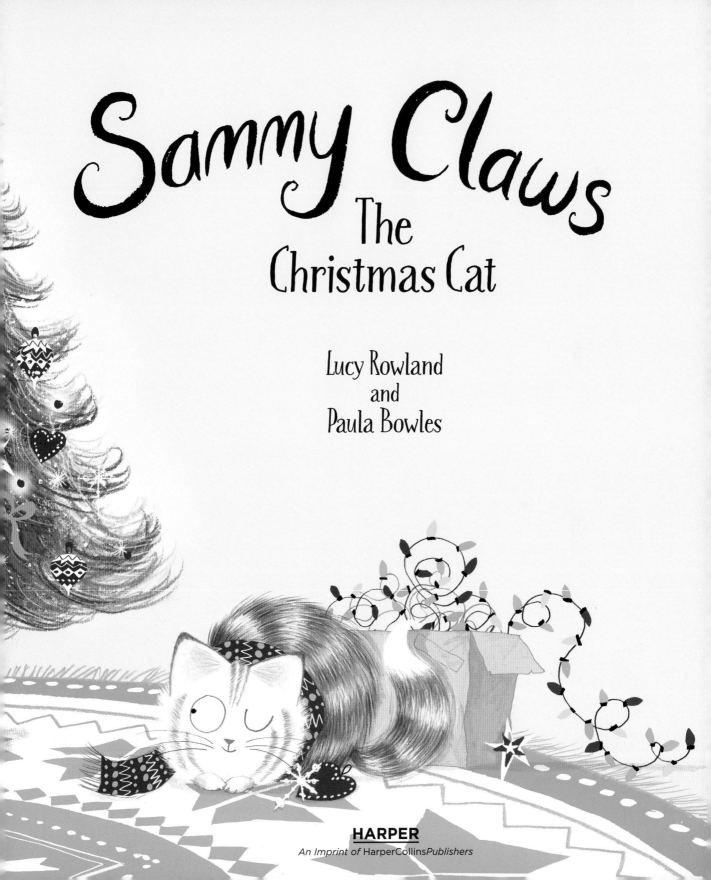

Sammy Claws
The Christmas Cat

Lucy Rowland
and
Paula Bowles

HARPER

An Imprint of HarperCollinsPublishers

Sleepy old Sammy Claws, Santa's pet cat,
was furry and purr-y and fluffy and fat.
He liked nothing better than having a **snooze**
in a box . . . or a cupboard . . . or snuggled in shoes.

And as Sammy dozed
he would **dream** of the day
that he'd travel with Santa
up high in his sleigh.

"Tomorrow is Christmas Eve!" Sammy Claws said.
He yawned a big yawn; then he curled up in bed.
"I'll help in the morning, then Santa Claus might
just take me along on his sleigh for the night!"

But . . .

23
December

To Santa

... when Sammy awoke,
      hours had passed!

"Am I too late to help?"
he cried, dashing off fast.

He ran to the workshop and leapt past the elves.
The door swung behind him…

ELF
&
SAFETY

and toppled the shelves!
The presents went flying –
oops! –
past Santa's head.

"Oh, Sammy,
we're busy!
WATCH OUT!"
Santa said.

Poor Sammy crept off and he looked rather sad.
"I wanted to help," he thought. "Now I feel bad.
I'm sure Santa won't let me fly with him now.
There must be a way to say sorry, but how?

RIBBON-O-MATIC

Perhaps while I think I'll just rest for a minute."
He found a big box ... and he slowly climbed in it.

OUT

The elves worked so hard. There was so much to do!
But sleepy old Sammy Claws hadn't a clue.
Sammy just wanted to doze for a while . . .

but his box was wrapped up
and then placed on a pile.

IN

Magic Dust
5.02

At six o'clock Santa was ready to go.
He jumped in the sleigh with a loud "Ho! Ho! Ho!"
He held the reins tightly, got ready to fly . . .

and off they all sped through the starry night sky.

Now, during the trip, they were going so fast
that Sammy woke up from his snooze at long last.
But what a surprise for poor Sammy the cat.
He was stuck in a box
with nowhere to scat!

He scrabbled around then he gave a loud shout . . .
but nobody heard . . . and he couldn't get out!

That night Santa worked
just as hard as could be.

(But still found some time for a cookie . . . or three.)

He hurried from mountain . . .

to seaside . . .

to town.

He found all the chimneys . . .
and quickly climbed down.

But in such a rush, with the lamplight so dim . . .
he didn't see two **robbers** waiting for him.
Their names were Bad Billy and Mischievous May.
They wanted to **steal** all the presents away!

They climbed on the sleigh
and they crouched really low
as Santa set off with his sack
through the snow.
"We'll grab 'em," said Billy,
"as soon as we can!"

But Sammy Claws heard every word of the plan.
"A plot to rob Santa? We'll see about that!
I'll soon stop those villains!" thought Sammy the cat.

Now, at a big castle (somewhere south of France),
as Santa set off, May hissed, "Quick! Here's our chance!
Just **look** at those presents! That's **such** a big pile.
Delivering those will take Santa a while!"

"Let's **snatch** all these presents!"
said Bill with a scowl.

They reached for a box,

but ...

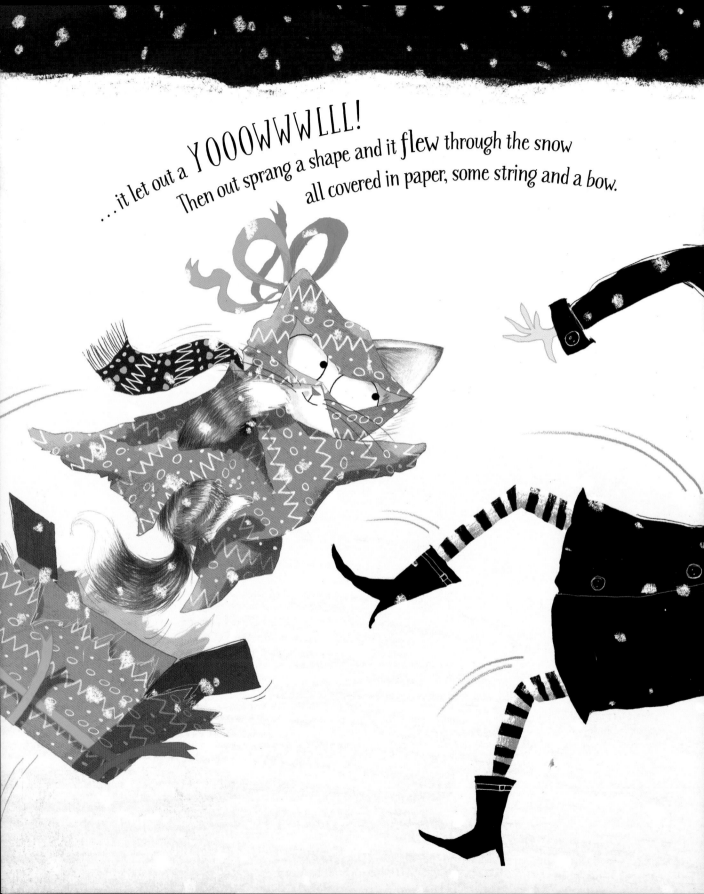

...it let out a YOOOWWWLLL!
Then out sprang a shape and it flew through the snow
all covered in paper, some string and a bow.

They fell in a snowdrift, headfirst, and – what luck! –
those mischievous robbers were both firmly stuck.
Police cars arrived on the scene with a wail
as Sammy looked on with a flick of his tail.

When Santa popped out of the chimney, "Ho! Ho . . .
Oh!" What was that down on the ground far below?
Two robbers? Police cars? And what a surprise . . .

"It's Sammy the cat!" Santa rubbed at his eyes.
"However did Sammy get all the way here?"
But as Santa wondered it soon became clear.

"You were wrapped in a present,
but then you broke free
and frightened those robbers away!
Now I see!"

He hugged Sammy tight
as they climbed in the sleigh.
"Oh, Sammy," said Santa,
"you've **saved** Christmas Day!

From now on," he promised,
"we'll work as a **team**!"
And Sammy Claws grinned.
This was his dream!

What fun they both had
as they worked through the night.
And as they flew home
Sammy closed his eyes tight.

He thought to himself,
"Oh, next year will be great!
Unless I'm too sleepy . . .

No! What if I'm late?"

But Santa had one last present, you see.
A brightly wrapped parcel sat under the tree.
And Santa was smiling.
They heard a tick -tock . . .

What was
Sammy's
present . . . ?

His own
ALARM CLOCK!